Fixing Gwen

A Drama

Sam Bobrick

MUSIC USE NOTE

Licensees are solely responsible for obtaining formal written permission from copyright owners to use copyrighted music in the performance of this play and are strongly cautioned to do so. If no such permission is obtained by the licensee, then the licensee must use only original music that the licensee owns and controls. Licensees are solely responsible and liable for all music clearances and shall indemnify the copyright owners of the play(s) and their licensing agent, Samuel French, against any costs, expenses, losses and liabilities arising from the use of music by licensees. Please contact the appropriate music licensing authority in your territory for the rights to any incidental music.

IMPORTANT BILLING AND CREDIT REQUIREMENTS

If you have obtained performance rights to this title, please refer to your licensing agreement for important billing and credit requirements.

FIXING GWEN was first presented as a staged reading at Theatre West on January 20, 2013 in Los Angeles, CA. The performance was directed by Susan Morgenstern. The cast was as follows:

MARK MORTON . . . . John Cygan

DANNY MORTON . . . . Joey Jennings

YOUNG GWEN . . . . Heidi Brucker

OLDER GWEN . . . . .Jeanine Anderson

CHARACTERS

MARK MORTON – A man in his early 50s
DANNY MORTON – **MARK**'s 16, going on 17, year old son
YOUNG GWEN – **MARK**'s wife when he first married her, early 20s
OLDER GWEN – **MARK**'s wife as she is now, late 40s

TIME

The Present

PLACE

A motel room in Palm Springs

ACT I

Scene One

(TIME: The Present. A Spring Evening.)

(PLACE: The entire play takes place in a moderately priced, comfortably decorated, ground floor motel room in Palm Springs, California. The entrance is downstage right. On the wall next to it is a light switch for the overhead lighting. A bathroom door is at upstage right. Along the stage right wall is a closet with a sliding door or a free standing wardrobe. At upstage center are two twin beds separated by a bedside table with a phone and lamp on it. Two small matching dressers are on the other sides of the beds. Upstage left is an easy chair. Downstage left is a sliding glass door that opens to a patio with two plastic bushes. On the bed at stage right is a medium sized structured suitcase. On the floor at the foot of the other bed at stage left is a nylon duffel bag. Leaning against that bed is a guitar case.)

(AT RISE: **DANNY MORTON** *a sixteen, going on seventeen, year old boy in jeans and a current rock band t-shirt lies on the bed with his hands behind his head staring into space. His sneakers are still on. We hear the toilet flush, the sink being turned on, then off. The bathroom door opens and* **MARK MORTON**, *a man in his early fifties, wearing slacks and a sweater enters the room, wiping his hands on a small hand towel. He stares at his son* **DANNY** *for a moment and then proceeds to the bed and his suitcase.)*

MARK. This isn't so bad. Pleasantly decorated. Somewhat clean rugs. Only moderately stained bedspreads. Not bad for a hundred and eighty bucks a night. Unfortunately we're paying two hundred and eighty bucks a night so I guess it is a little bit of a screw job. But it's the nearest place to the hospital so we won't be spending time in traffic.

*(***DANNY*** doesn't respond. ***MARK*** tosses his hand towel on the edge of his bed and begins to unpack still trying to make conversation.)*

I hope you don't mind my taking the bed closest to the bathroom. At my age it's a necessity. No, this place isn't bad at all for what it is. By the way, since there's no room service they do give you a free breakfast, most likely juice, coffee and rolls which is usually all I have anyway, but if you feel like pancakes or something more substantial, I saw a couple of nice restaurants down the street so food shouldn't be a problem. I suppose they'll have lunch for us at the hospital, which if it's like all the other hospital food I've eaten, will put you in the hospital.

(Waiting for a response from his joke. There is none. He sighs.)

Do you want to unpack?

DANNY. *(Annoyed but not angry)* I don't know how the fuck I let you talk me into coming down here.

MARK. How? Because you're a sixteen year old teenager and I let you drive my new Lexus here, that's why. By the way, I was very impressed with your driving. In the hundred and twenty miles you were behind the wheel we only had three near fatal collisions. Not bad for a first year driver. When Brian and Wendy began driving they were nightmares. Look, it's not going to be that bad here. Six days, that's all it is. They think it's just as important for families to learn how to deal with the situation as it is for the person with the problem. Next Sunday morning we'll be on our way home. Besides, this could actually be a good bonding experience for us. You know we never really get to spend that much time together. My being out of town as much as I have to be and you being caught up with your life, school, friends and whatever else keeps you away from the house, so I hardly ever see you. Anyway, I really appreciate you coming down here with me. I'm just sorry your brother and sister didn't come.

DANNY. Why would they? They hate her guts.

MARK. No. That's not it. Brian has two big trials that he needs to prepare for and Wendy's boss wouldn't give her the time off.

DANNY. Dad, let's get real. They both could have gotten away if they wanted to. They didn't because they want nothing to do with her anymore and as you know I'm not that fond of mommie dearest myself.

MARK. Yeah. I know. You told me. Many times. But after she gets all fixed up I'm sure you'll all change your minds.

DANNY. Fixed up to what?

MARK. To what she was when I first married her. Before she got caught up with the wine and the pills. She was really very different. She was actually wonderful.

DANNY. Yeah, so you keep telling us.

MARK. Well, she was. That's why I fell in love with her. Beautiful, bright, sweet… You ought to look at some of the early pictures of her when we first got married. She was really something special.

DANNY. I only know her as she is now. A mean, miserable drunk who's been that way since I can remember. And that's the way Brian and Wendy know her too. They couldn't wait until they were old enough to get out of the house and neither can I. It seems you're the only one with any good memories of this very fucked up human being.

MARK. I know. But take my word for it. She was once totally different and once they get her situation under control, I know we're gonna get that person back.

*(**DANNY** rises, throws his bag on the bed and begins unpacking.)*

DANNY. Jesus Christ, Dad. Sometimes you are so clueless. You may be a hot shot in the business world but when it comes to facing the truth about that woman, you are on another planet. Nothing's going to change her because nothing has, nothing can and nothing will. Not therapy, not your screaming, not your begging, nothing. Why? Because she doesn't want to change. She's very happy with her miserable boozed up life just the way it is. Brian can see it. Wendy can see it. I can see it. Only you can't see it.

MARK. I think you're wrong about that. She agreed to go into rehab. That was something.

DANNY. She agreed because she drove her car into a fucking convenience store with a blood alcohol level high enough to kill an elephant. It was either go to rehab or go to jail.

MARK. That's not quite true. My lawyer could have gotten her off and can still get her off but we thought this was the best thing for her. Look, she's your mother, she's my wife. Let's at least stay hopeful. I've seen her the last three weekends since she's been down here and you're going to be amazed how much better she looks. Not so puffy and I think a lot less angry. I could actually sense that sweetness she once had coming back. I think you're going to be in for a pleasant surprise.

DANNY. When it comes to my mother, the word "pleasant" has no business ever being used. As far as surprises go, I'll be surprised when you finally realize she's never going to be what you want her to be or even what you thought she was.

MARK. *(Finally angered)* I know what she was, okay? I know damn well, what she was. I'm not backing down from that. So lay off that. Damn it!

(Calming down)

I'm sorry. Sometimes the negativity in this family drives me up a wall.

DANNY. I'm not negative. I'm just saying there's not a chance in hell anything good is going to come from her being here.

MARK. Okay, you made your point.

(DANNY*'s cell phone rings. He takes it out of his pocket, checks to see who's calling. He perks up a bit.)*

DANNY. Sorry, dad. Gotta take this one. It's Jenny. We're sort of going together.

MARK. Oh? I didn't know you were going with anyone. When do I get to meet her?

(**MARK** *continues to unpack.* **DANNY** *lies back on his bed.)*

DANNY. Hopefully not for a while. I'm trying to keep her away from the house as long as I can.

(On cell)

Hi, Jen. How's it going? Yeah, I miss you too. No, it wasn't bad at all. I drove all the way so it didn't seem so long. Yeah, his Lexus drove very nicely. I wouldn't want one, but I guess it makes sense for someone over fifty.

(**MARK** *reacts.)*

What? Sure.

(To **MARK***)*

Jenny says "hi".

MARK. That's nice. Tell her "hi" back.

DANNY. He says "hi" back. Yeah, I miss you too. I thought I just told you that. How much? Jesus, I've only been gone five hours. How much can a guy miss a girl in five hours? At least give me till morning. So what's going on?… It still hasn't, huh. Well, you know, your period has always been strange.

(**MARK** *looks up shocked. This has really caught his attention.)*

DANNY. *(cont.)* Come on, don't worry. We had this scare before and it always works out. Look, can I call you back later. I think my dad is about to have a stroke. Yeah, I miss you too. I'm sure I'll be able to tell you how much in the next call. Bye.

(He sends her a kiss and puts the phone away.)

Nice girl but possessive as hell.

MARK. *(Incredulous)* She missed her period?

DANNY. *(No big deal)* Yeah, it's a week late. It's nothing to sweat about, trust me. It's happened a couple times before.

MARK. You… You're having sex?

DANNY. Yeah. So?

MARK. You're not even seventeen.

DANNY. I will be in a couple of weeks.

MARK. How old is she?

DANNY. About the same. Besides, what does age have to do with sex? It's strictly a biological thing. You're ready for it when you're ready for it. Jenny and I were ready for it about eight months ago. Besides, these are supposed to be a guy's best sexual years. Why waste them?

MARK. Why? Why? I don't know why, but I'm sure given time I'll come up with something. I had no idea you were…were having… I'm really thrown.

DANNY. Oh, come on, dad. Like I suppose you didn't have sex when you were my age.

MARK. Yeah, well, no. I was at least a year older. I'm almost sure of it. And a year's a big difference in a teenager's development. One year is like…like two or three years in an adult.

DANNY. You mean sort of like dog years.

MARK. Exactly.

(Shaking his head in disbelief)

She missed her period?

DANNY. I told you. It's nothing to sweat about. She's on the pill.

MARK. At sixteen?

DANNY. It helps with her acne.

MARK. Are you two very serious about each other?

DANNY. Well, yes and no.

MARK. Maybe you can be a little more specific.

DANNY. Well, we're serious for now, while we're in high school but we're both smart enough to know we may not be that serious for what comes after high school. Right now we're just a couple of young, immature, horny kids and it's kind of unrealistic at our age to commit to one person this soon, don't you think?

MARK. I think this conversation may be a little too grown-up for me. Do your brother and sister know you're having sex?

DANNY. Why should I tell them?

MARK. Because they're your sibs. They may have some good advice for you.

DANNY. Good advice? You mean like different positions?

MARK. No. I mean like maybe it's too early for you and… and this Jenny to be…so involved in something like this. I'd really feel better if you talked to them.

DANNY. I don't know what you think they're going to tell me. I don't know about Wendy, but Brian was having sex when he was even younger than me.

MARK. Oh, God!

DANNY. For crying out loud, Dad. It's only sex. It's not that big a deal.

MARK. I happen to think it is.

DANNY. Well, I guess that's a generational thing. But my generation has no problem with it.

MARK. What about your mother? Does she know?

DANNY. Why would she care what I do? Half the time she doesn't even know when I'm in the same room with her.

MARK. *(He nods, puzzled.)* You know what? I have no idea what I'm supposed to say right now.

DANNY. Why do you think you have to say anything? I think it all makes perfect sense.

MARK. To you, yes. To me, no. Damn it, it's my duty as a parent to see that my children are walking the right path. It's seems I haven't been as diligent about that as I should have been.

DANNY. How could you be? Between your working and your traveling and your trying to deal with a maniac at home, you've had your hands full. Besides, it's a little late to get concerned. I'm the only one left at home and unfortunately I'm pretty set in my ways now.

MARK. Yeah, well, that's too bad because once this problem with your mother gets taken care of there's going to be some un-setting of your ways.

DANNY. No, I don't think there will and I'll tell you why. Mom's going to go right back to drinking, you'll go right back to trying to fix her and I'll go right back to counting the days I have left living in our supremely fucked up house.

MARK. Look, do you have to use the "F" word so much? It's really starting to annoy me.

DANNY. Come on, Dad, that's how teenagers talk. It's a very normal part of conversation. Besides, it's a great word. It seems to describe everything perfectly.

(Teasing)

The fucking Dodgers, the fucking Lakers, I'm fucked, you're fucked, holy fuck and best of all, let's fuck. It fits anywhere. I don't know what I'd do without it. You ought to try using it. Make it your fucking friend. You'll fucking love it. You'll see. It makes life a lot fucking easier.

MARK. *(Nods. A beat.)* I may have made a big mistake not getting separate rooms for us. Look, right now my head is on overload. Let's go grab something to eat or go to a movie or drive my car off a bridge, but let's get the hell out of here before I become anymore enlightened about what the hell else is going on in your life. We can finish unpacking later.

DANNY. Yeah, fine. By the way, this little talk we're having, is this what you mean by bonding?

MARK. I'm not sure. But if it is, it's highly over rated.

(Opens door)

Come on. If we do go to a movie, please, let's pick one without any teenagers in it. She missed her period. Holy fuck!

(DANNY *and* **MARK** *exit.* **MARK** *closes the door behind them.)*

(Blackout)

Scene Two

(TIME: The middle of the night. The room is dimly lit from the moonlight.)

*(***DANNY*** is asleep in his bed. **MARK**, in pajama bottoms and an undershirt is sitting at the end of his bed staring blankly ahead. A beautiful woman, in a white nightgown is sitting in the easy chair. This is **YOUNG GWEN**, **MARK**'s wife in her early twenties. Both stare ahead, neither speaking directly to the other. This is a dream and they are both lit appropriately.)*

YOUNG GWEN. You still love me don't you?

MARK. Of course I do. Why do you even ask?

YOUNG GWEN. I need to know. You were so much in love, weren't you?

MARK. Very much in love.

YOUNG GWEN. Is it the same kind of love now.

MARK. Of course it is.

YOUNG GWEN. I've changed you know. I'm not the same person.

MARK. But you will be again. I promise you. You will be again.

YOUNG GWEN. And I'll be happy this time won't I?

MARK. Very happy.

YOUNG GWEN. And the children?

MARK. They'll be happy too.

YOUNG GWEN. I really wanted our lives to be happy. I really did. You do believe that, don't you?

MARK. Of course I do.

YOUNG GWEN. I'm sorry, Mark. I'm truly sorry.

MARK. I know.

YOUNG GWEN. Tell the children, please tell the children. I did not want it to turn out this way.

MARK. I'll tell them.

YOUNG GWEN. Am I still beautiful, Mark?

MARK. Yes. Yes you are.

YOUNG GWEN. And sweet.

MARK. Yes. Very sweet.

YOUNG GWEN. Just the way I was when you fell in love with me.

MARK. Exactly the way.

YOUNG GWEN. I will be that person again, Mark. I promise. I'll be that person again. You'll see.

MARK. I know you will. And it will be wonderful again, Gwen. It will be so wonderful again.

YOUNG GWEN. Yes. All so wonderful again.

MARK. Yes. Just the way it was. Exactly the way it was.

(The lights fade to black.)

Scene Three

(TIME: Same day. Early evening.)

*(**DANNY**, wearing jeans and a Budweiser beer t-shirt, is on his cell phone and walking around the room.)*

DANNY. Hey, Jen. Sorry I couldn't take your call. They made us shut off our phones. How was it? Well, it didn't start off so good. We spent most of the day learning how to deal with the alcoholic in the family and I guess I was pissing the staff off because instead of using the word "alcoholic", I kept using the word "drunk". They finally told me that out of respect I need to use the word "alcoholic" instead of "drunk" which I really tried doing but wasn't always successful. Then I guess I pissed them off a little more by falling asleep a lot and then at the end of the day I think I pissed them off a little more when they asked us what we thought about the program so far and I raised my hand and told them that as far as my mother was concerned they were wasting their fucking time. Yeah, I did say "fucking" but I didn't mean to. I also said "fucking drunks" a couple of times too, but I think by then they had given up on me.

Anyway, it seems what pissed them off the most was what I wore. See, most of the staff is made up of recovering drunks... I mean alcoholics and I didn't realize it would be an issue, but I wore a t-shirt with a picture of a can of Budweiser on the front. Yeah, I know it's one of your favs, But it apparently wasn't one of theirs. Anyway they asked me not to wear it again and I said "sure" and then I realized that all I brought along with me was my Miller Lite t-shirt, my Jack Daniels t-shirt and three others praising the benefits of marijuana. Yeah, they're really a bunch of tight asses. Anyway, my dad is out buying me some new ones. My mother? Yeah, I saw her but basically all I got to say was hello.

My dad had lunch with her but I had to eat alone. Except for the spouses who have been coming up every weekend, they keep the rest of the family away from them for a day or two until we've been properly indoctrinated. You get the feeling you're visiting a jailed convict, which is the only good feeling I've had since I've been up here.

Yeah, I could have eaten with some of the other dudes there but to tell you the truth, they looked more fucked up than the drunk they were visiting. Ooops, alcoholic. Anyway my dad and I are having lunch with her tomorrow. I've never seen her eat a meal without a glass of wine in front of her. It should be very interesting.

(**MARK**, *wearing slacks, shirt and light jacket enters with a bag of T-shirts.*)

*(To **MARK**)* I'm talking to Jen.

MARK. Oh. Did her friend come to visit?

DANNY. Her what?

MARK. Her friend. That's the term we used in my day when a girl got her P-E-R-I-O-D.

(Obviously Jen heard him over the phone.)

DANNY. She said N-O. She didn't G-E-T it yet.

MARK. She didn't. Tell her S-H-I-T.

DANNY. *(On phone)* You heard. Yeah, sometimes he is cute. Look, I'll call you later tonight. Yeah, I miss you too. Bye.

(Puts cell phone away)

MARK. *(Takes off jacket)* I got you six t-shirts. There wasn't much of a choice. Some of them were pretty vulgar. They actually had one that said "Go Fuck Yourself".

DANNY. Cool. I hope you bought it.

MARK. No. I got Super heroes. That shouldn't offend anyone.

(Takes them out of the bag)

MARK. *(cont.)* I got two Superman, two Batman and two Wonder Woman.

DANNY. Wonder Woman?

MARK. I told you, there wasn't much of a choice.

DANNY. I can't wear Wonder Woman.

MARK. Sure you can. I think it makes a very important and admirable statement for a guy in today's world.

DANNY. Yeah. That he's a pussy. I really don't like any of them.

(He puts the T-shirts aside.)

MARK. Well, you can't wear the t-shirts you brought. Please, for me, tomorrow wear one of these shirts.

DANNY. I'll think about it. That's the best I can do right now.

MARK. I'm asking for a favor Danny.

DANNY. Okay, okay. I'll wear one.

MARK. Thanks. Now for dinner we can do one of two things. We can go to some joint around here or we can send out for a pizza or something. I found a bunch of restaurant menus in my drawer.

DANNY. Pizza's great.

MARK. Good. Because I'm bushed.

(Pulls out a menu)

Here. Wong's Pizzeria. That should be interesting. I never had a Chinese pizza before.

(Takes out his cell and dials)

How does pepperoni sound to you?

DANNY. Perfect.

MARK. *(On Phone)* Hello, is this Wong? Oh, really?

(To **DANNY***)*

There is no Wong.

(On phone)

So why do you call it Wongs?

(To **DANNY***)*

It used to be a laundry and they wanted to keep the neon sign. It makes sense.

(On phone)

Well, look, I'm at the Colonial Inn, Room 127. I want a large pepperoni pizza and two large Cokes.

DANNY. Listen, Dad, since I've been a good sport about coming up here can I have a beer?

MARK. *(On phone)* Hold it, Wong or whatever your name is.

(To **DANNY***)*

A beer? You drink beer? Since when do you drink beer?

DANNY. Since I started having sex. They go well together.

MARK. Oh, shit.

DANNY. That was a joke. Come on, be a sport. It was a rough day and I think a beer would do us both good.

MARK. I'm not sure it's the right thing to do. Especially while we're going through this rehab stuff. I had no idea you drank.

DANNY. I don't drink. I'm like you. Once in a while I like to have a beer. That's not drinking. Trust me. A lot of kids my age are into a lot worse things.

MARK. And you're not?

DANNY. No. I've learned all too well from my beloved mother's condition how disgusting you look walking around bombed out of your gourd. Besides, I like pot a lot better. That just makes you mellow

MARK. Oh great!

DANNY. Kidding Dad. I swear I'm just kidding. Jesus, what happened to your sense of humor dad?

MARK. I lost it somewhere between your girlfriend missing her period and the t-shirt that said "Go Fuck Yourself". Man, if I leave here without a heart attack it will be a miracle. Okay. One beer, just this once.

DANNY. What a guy.

MARK. *(Gets back on the phone)* Hello Wong. Thanks for holding. Scratch the Cokes and make it two beers. You don't? Well, for a ten buck tip can you stop and pick up a couple of Buds or something. Good. See you soon.

(Hangs up)

DANNY. Thanks Dad. Every now and then you're the coolest.

MARK. Thank you. I just hope I'm not the dumbest.

(Sits on bed and kicks off his shoes)

So what did you think of the day?

DANNY. For you, I guess it was good. For me, truthfully, I could have lived without it

MARK. Really? Too bad. I think this week here is going to be the best thing that ever happened to this family.

DANNY. What family? There's just you and me.

MARK. Maybe if you stayed awake during the orientation you would have heard that her recovery is going to affect everyone whether they're here or not. For the first time I feel hopeful. These people seem to know what they're doing and the success rate is impressive. I just wish Brian and Wendy had come along. They definitely could have benefited from this.

DANNY. You think so?

MARK. Sure they would. They would have learned that your mother's condition is not a choice. I'm not sure they're aware of that. I wasn't. There's some flaw in her genetic structure that doesn't allow her to stop drinking once she starts.

DANNY. You may see it as a flaw. I think she sees it as winning the lottery.

MARK. Look, lose the sarcasm. Maybe if you tried staying awake tomorrow you'll see things a little more clearly and with a little more compassion.

DANNY. I see things clearly enough and I'm not going through this week with blinders on and the false hope that you have. Do you know what you're going to get from this week?

MARK. I can hardly wait to hear.

DANNY. Disappointment. Wake up, Dad, that woman knows damn well what she's doing. Think about it. There hasn't been a morning that I can remember that she hasn't staggered out of your bedroom looking like the bride of Frankenstein. And always promising us that this time she learned her lesson and she's had her last drink. Three hours later she's got a wine glass in her hand and back to being a drunken lunatic.

MARK. But that's just it. She couldn't do it by herself. Now she's getting the tools to help her stay sober.

DANNY. The only tool she's going to work with when she gets home is a corkscrew. For Christ's sake, Dad, she's been the way she is ever since any of us kids can remember and why you've put up with it as long as you have is something none of us understand.

MARK. Because I was sure that one day I'd be able to get her to beat this thing. I feel very positive about this program working for her and so does she. We're going to get this family of ours back on track, you'll see.

DANNY. Family, family! Please stop using that word. There is no family. There hasn't been a family in our house for years. Thanks to her, no one shows up for Thanksgiving, no one shows up for Christmas, no one shows up for anything anymore. Think! When was the last time Brian and his wife and kids came over the house? Months go by without seeing them and they live twenty minutes away. Wendy only comes by when she needs to hit you up for money.

MARK. Things are going to be different this time, Danny. You'll see.

DANNY. No. I won't see. I won't ever see and you're just going to keep pissing the rest of your life away trying to change someone that can't be changed and I don't know why.

MARK. Maybe it's called loyalty.

DANNY. Loyalty? What the hell is there to be loyal about? She was never a mother and I don't think she was much of a wife either. Brian, Wendy and me, we were all raised by housekeepers that kept coming and going because they couldn't stand her either. Until I was five, I spoke better Spanish than English. Until I was five I didn't know who the hell my mother was. I can't tell you how disappointed I was when I found out it was her.

MARK. I know at times it was very tough for you kids.

DANNY. Not at times, Dad. It's been tough every single day we lived with that woman. Do you really have any idea what our growing up was like with her? We couldn't make noise, We couldn't put on lights cause it hurt her eyes. We couldn't have friends over to the house. She'd call us names, tell us we were imbeciles, monsters, ungrateful, spoiled rotten brats that she should have aborted. Our happiest times with her was when she'd be passed out. Before we had housekeepers, Brian told me how she'd lock him and Wendy in their rooms for hours and you know why? Not because they did anything wrong, but because she'd be able to drink and not have to deal with them.

MARK. *(Disbelief)* They never said anything to me about that.

DANNY. Because they were little kids. They thought it was normal. Besides, anytime any of us tried to tell you what was happening, you'd make up some lame excuse for her. Then she'd be pissed at us for ratting her out.

MARK. I was just trying to calm things down. I work long hours, I'm out of town a lot.

DANNY. That woman would be mean just to be mean. I'm going to tell you something and I hope you don't take it the wrong way. Things got so bad, that when you two would take an airplane trip together, we actually hoped the plane would go down.

MARK. That's pretty harsh.

DANNY. I know. We knew we'd miss you, but we despised her so much we thought it was worth the trade off. She was our enemy, Dad, not our mother, our enemy.

MARK. You're really picking a bad time to unload.

DANNY. Maybe it's because I finally have the chance to do it. Goddamn it, Dad, our lives have been total crap and yours is going to remain crap as long as you keep waiting for a stupid miracle that is never going to come.

MARK. My life may seem difficult, but it's not been total crap.

DANNY. Oh, come on, Dad. She's screaming at you all the time.

MARK. It's not that bad. I'm able to handle it.

DANNY. Really? Well then I guess what they say is true. When you're up to your neck in shit every day, you get used to the smell.

MARK. Terrific. And where did that bit of twisted wisdom come from?

DANNY. One of my t-shirts that I'm sorry I didn't bring with me.

MARK. Next week when I come back here to take her home, I honestly believe I'll be taking home a very changed woman.

DANNY. If that happens, you probably have the wrong woman in your car. So help me, at this point I'd be more than satisfied if she came home at least a happy drunk. I mean it. I've got a couple of friends whose parents are alcoholics too. But they're happy alcoholics. They load up and until they pass out, they're laughing and smiling and except for falling down stairs now and then, are actually quite pleasant. I could live with that. For Mother's Day I'd even be willing to spring for a keg of beer.

MARK. Danny, this is an important effort your mother is making.

DANNY. Dad, you're a good guy and I know you mean well. I'll be out of school in a year and then I'm gone. But if this doesn't turn out the way you want it to, maybe it's time to give up the dream and take care of yourself. It's what Brian would like for you, it's what Wendy would like for you, it's what I would like for you. Would you at least promise me that?

MARK. Look, can we put this discussion on hold until after she's back home when we can see more clearly how things are going. I don't know how many times I have to say this, but I know it's going to be different.

DANNY. *(Frustrated)* I've been talking to a rock, haven't I? Nothing I've said got through to you, did it? Nothing. Sometimes I wonder who's crazier, you or her.

You have made up your mind to keep going down the drain with her and that's that. Well, screw it and fuck it all. Tomorrow I'm wearing my Miller Lite t-shirt to the hospital and if they don't like it, they can all kiss my ass.

(Throws himself down on his bed)

Where the fuck is the pizza?

*(**MARK** sits down on his bed, takes a deep breath and a long pause.)*

MARK. So what else impressed you about today?

(Lights fade to black.)

Scene Four

(TIME: The middle of the night. The room is dimly lit from the moonlight.)

*(**MARK** is asleep in his bed. **DANNY**, in boxer shorts, sits at the edge of his bed staring blankly ahead. His area is lit a little brighter. **OLDER GWEN**, a woman in her late forties, in a white nightgown, stands near him, looking at him. It's obvious that although she was beautiful at a younger age, and that some of that beauty still seeps through, alcohol has not been kind to her. She holds a bottle of wine in one hand and a wine glass in the other and pours a drink. She has a bit of a buzz on.)*

OLDER GWEN. You don't think I can do it, do you?

DANNY. No, I don't.

OLDER GWEN. Well, I can.

DANNY. I don't think so. You are what you are. A raving, psychotic drunk.

OLDER GWEN. I'm your mother.

DANNY. A raving, psychotic drunk who happens to be my mother.

OLDER GWEN. You're so cruel to me. Why are you so cruel to me? You know I love you. I love you the most. Certainly more than the others.

DANNY. No, you don't. You don't love anyone. Not me, not Brian, not Wendy, not Dad. I doubt you even love yourself. Your love is the bottle of wine you're drinking and the handful of pills you're taking.

OLDER GWEN. I'm in pain, Danny. Can't you see, I'm in pain?

DANNY. And I suppose you think we're not? But it's always about you, isn't it? What the world has done to you. You and only you. You, the constant victim. Well, you aren't the goddamn victim. We are. Three kids who had to live in a fucking nightmare with you.

OLDER GWEN. You heard your father. I'm going to change, Danny. I'm going to be a good mother, a good wife. Everything everyone wants me to be. I told your father I will and I will.

DANNY. I don't care if you do or you don't. Not anymore. My father is a fool and one fool in the family is enough.

OLDER GWEN. Why can't you be kind to me? No one is kind to me.

DANNY. Me, me, me! There it is again. Do you ever think about anyone besides yourself? You're pathetic. You know, at first I felt sorry for you. Then I felt shame. Now I just don't give a damn. For all I care, you can drink yourself straight to hell. Maybe you've done that already.

OLDER GWEN. If I wasn't so unhappy it would have been different. If only I wasn't so unhappy.

DANNY. Unhappy about what? Goddamn it, about what? You have a nice home, you have security, a husband who for some sick reason keeps hangin' in…

OLDER GWEN. You're not my friends. None of you care about me. None of you. I'm so unhappy.

(Pouring another drink)

I'm so very unhappy.

(During the following, **OLDER GWEN** *turns and slowly drifts towards downstage left.)*

DANNY. *(Mocking)* Unhappy, unhappy, unhappy.

(Suddenly he rises, goes to her and turns her around to face him.)

You're always "so unhappy". About what? About what?

OLDER GWEN. So unhappy.

(She turns and, walking away slowly, disappears into the black, exiting through the downstage left sidelines. **DANNY** *is left standing there.)*

DANNY. *(Raising his voice)* Unhappy about what? About what? Goddamn it, unhappy about what?

*(**DANNY**'s ranting wakes **MARK**. He turns on his bedside lamp, gets out of bed and begins shaking **DANNY**.)*

About what? About what? Unhappy about what?

MARK. Danny! Danny!

DANNY. About what? About what? Goddamn it, about what? About what?

MARK. Danny!

*(**DANNY** awakens.)*

DANNY. Huh? What?

MARK. You were dreaming.

DANNY. I was. Yeah.

MARK. Are you alright?

DANNY. Yeah, yeah. I… I'm fine.

MARK. Do you want to talk about it?

DANNY. No.

MARK. Are you sure?

DANNY. Yes.

MARK. *(Looks at him for a moment)* Okay. Try to get some sleep. We have an early day.

DANNY. Yeah, sure.

*(**MARK** leads **DANNY** back to his bed. **DANNY** gets under the covers.)*

(A beat) Dad?

MARK. Yes?

DANNY. What made her so unhappy? Do you know?

MARK. *(Sighs)* Try to get some sleep.

*(**DANNY** lies down and falls right to sleep. **MARK** looks at his son for several beats then returns to his bed. He turns off the bedside lamp and sits on his bed. The moonlight now illuminates his area. A light comes up revealing **YOUNG GWEN** standing behind **MARK**.)*

(She begins rubbing his shoulders, slowly, tenderly. He doesn't turn to face her.)

YOUNG GWEN. You know why I'm so unhappy, don't you Mark?

MARK. *(Hesitant)* Yes.

YOUNG GWEN. Then why don't you tell him.

MARK. I'm not sure he'd understand.

YOUNG GWEN. I think he would.

MARK. It wouldn't change things.

YOUNG GWEN. Maybe not. But at least he'd understand.

MARK. Damn it. Aren't things screwed up enough?

YOUNG GWEN. *(Sits next to him)* Do you regret any of it, Mark?

MARK. *(Looks at her for a beat then strokes her hair)* No. Not for a moment.

YOUNG GWEN. Our lives would have been so different.

MARK. Maybe.

YOUNG GWEN. Of course they would have been. We both know they would have been. Maybe this would never have happened to me, to any of us.

MARK. Our lives are going to be fine, Gwen. They were once and they will be again. I promise you, they will be again.

YOUNG GWEN. It's comforting to believe that, isn't it?

MARK. I have to believe that Gwen. I have to.

(Lights slowly fade to black.)

Scene Five

(TIME: Later that day. Early evening.)

*(***DANNY*** *is on his bed strumming his guitar. He is wearing a Miller Lite t-shirt. He seems very reflective. The motel door opens and* ***MARK*** *enters. He's wearing a different shirt under his jacket. He is very solemn. He looks at* ***DANNY***, *then shakes his head and sighs.* ***DANNY*** *does not look up.)*

DANNY. You're pissed at me, aren't you?

MARK. What do you think?

DANNY. It was just as much her fault as it was mine.

MARK. Look, you made up your mind to be an asshole the minute you woke up.

DANNY. That's not true.

MARK. I told you not to wear that damn t-shirt.

DANNY. It's not the same t-shirt. Yesterday's was a Budweiser, today it's a Miller Lite. The taste is miles apart. Besides, I told you I didn't feel like being Batman or Superman and I certainly didn't feel like being Wonder Woman.

MARK. Sometimes in life you do things you don't want to do.

DANNY. Well, I didn't want to come here but I did.

MARK. I'm now wondering if that might have been a mistake.

DANNY. You want me to go home, I'll go home. There are buses leaving here all the time.

MARK. No, I don't want you to go home.

DANNY. Why not? That woman and I are never going to get along. What did they say after I left?

MARK. They were very understanding. They said things like this happen. They think you need to come back tomorrow.

DANNY. She threw her tray of food at me. She had hot coffee and hot soup. I feel sorry for the poor guy in back of me she actually hit. How the hell did that finally end up?

MARK. I apologized, offered to pay for his dry cleaning and promised to send him a gift certificate to a pricey restaurant. He was okay with that.

DANNY. So help me, dad, I tried. I really tried. You heard me at the beginning. I told her how good she looked. I told her how the dogs missed her at home. I told her how nice it would be to have her back again. I lied like I never lied before. It's a wonder my nose didn't bust through a wall.

MARK. I was very proud of you.

DANNY. Then when you left to go to the bathroom she started talking about all the people there that were ten times worse than her and about all the people who came up to her and said they didn't understand why she was there. She didn't believe for one minute she needed to be there. Once again she was the innocent victim. Once again nothing was her fault.

Well, I couldn't take one more minute of her bullshit, so for her own good, I decided to remind her why she was there. "It's because you're a full blown, fall down, fucking drunk who drove her fucking car into a fucking convenience store, that's why." So help me, I had no idea she'd be so offended. Then she started crying and yelling hysterically that I should be more supportive, that no one knows what she's going through. I've heard all that crap before and I wasn't in the mood to hear it again so I just left and walked back here. I don't know why the hell they want me to come back. I'm probably the last person in the world she wants to see.

MARK. She's not the reason they want you to come back. You're the reason they want you to come back. You have issues and you need to deal with them or it will jeopardize the success of her recovery.

DANNY. Success. If I hear that word again I'm going to throw up. There is not going to be success with that woman. Why can't anyone but me see that?

MARK. Look, I'm not fooling myself. This is not going to be easy. When she gets out of here there's still a long way to go. They want her to attend thirty AA meetings in thirty days.

DANNY. Thirty meetings? Her? No way that's gonna happen.

MARK. Yes it will happen. I'm going to take time off from work and go with her.

DANNY. You're going to be her policeman?

MARK. No. I'm going to be her husband.

DANNY. Why, Dad? Why do you hang in? At least tell me that?

(**MARK** *sighs, takes off his jacket and sits.*)

MARK. I once read that every one has one big love in their life and that's all. Whether that's true or not, for me it was. Your mother was mine. It's just that simple.

DANNY. Great. I've got one problem with that. What makes you think you were hers?

(*An awkward beat*)

I'm sorry Dad. It was just something I thought was smart to say.

MARK. I can't let her go, Danny. I can't.

DANNY. Even though she's not the same person you fell in love with?

MARK. Even though.

DANNY. I still don't get it.

(*Shakes his head. He feels he has to do something. He's not sure what.*)

Okay. I'll go back to the hospital with you tomorrow. I'll apologize to her. I'll apologize to everyone. I'll wear my Wonder Woman T-shirt. How's that?

MARK. (*Still very solemn*) I would appreciate it very much.

(Sits on the bed and takes off his shoes)

DANNY. Done. Now what about dinner? I saw a hamburger place down the street. Maybe we should give it a try.

MARK. No. I'm really not hungry right now. Why don't you go. I think I need to lay down for a minute or two.

DANNY. Are you okay?

MARK. I'm fine.

DANNY. Are you sure?

MARK. Yes, I'm sure.

DANNY. Can I bring you back something?

MARK. No, thanks.

DANNY. You sure?

MARK. I'm sure. Do you need any money?

DANNY. No, I have plenty. Since Jen and I got into sex we spend a lot less money on entertainment.

MARK. Great.

DANNY. It was another joke. I could use a few bucks.

MARK. Thank God.

(Reaches in his pocket, takes out some bills and hands them to **DANNY**)

Here's twenty.

DANNY. Thanks. Be back in about half an hour.

MARK. Sure.

DANNY. Maybe you'd like to go out for a walk when I get back. I passed a little park a few blocks away.

MARK. Maybe.

DANNY. I'm really sorry I said what I did. About you not being her big love. It just seemed clever to say but it wasn't very nice. Maybe you've noticed, sometimes I'm a bit of a dick.

MARK. I've noticed.

*(***DANNY*** goes to the door then turns to* **MARK.**)

DANNY. Okay, you told me you can't leave her because she's your great love. But be honest. If you knew what you'd have to go through with her, would you do it all again?

MARK. I don't know. Maybe. Maybe not. What does it matter? You can't go back in time.

DANNY. I know. But isn't that what you've been trying to do?

(**DANNY** *exits.* **MARK** *lies back on his bed and sighs.*)

(*Lights fade to black.*)

Scene Six

(TIME: The middle of the night. The room is dimly lit from the moonlight.)

*(***DANNY*** is under the covers. ***MARK****, in pajama bottoms and undershirt, is sitting on his bed. ***OLDER GWEN*** is nearby.)*

OLDER GWEN. You didn't tell him everything. You need to tell him everything.

MARK. I can't. Not yet.

OLDER GWEN. It would make a difference. I know it would.

MARK. Maybe.

OLDER GWEN. It would make a difference to me. He'd finally see why I am the way I am. Maybe he wouldn't hate me so much.

MARK. Maybe he would, maybe he wouldn't.

OLDER GWEN. I know he wouldn't. He'd finally understand. Brian and Wendy would too. Please, Mark, please. Tell him.

*(***MARK*** doesn't respond.)*

You still love me, don't you?

MARK. Yes.

OLDER GWEN. Is it the same kind of love now?

*(***MARK*** doesn't answer.)*

Look at me, Mark. Is it the same kind of love now?

MARK. *(Looks up at her)* Yes. Of course it is. You know it is. You know it will always be.

OLDER GWEN. Are you sure?

MARK. *(Sighs helplessly)* Does it really matter to you? Does it?

OLDER GWEN. It's so sad, isn't it? To waste a life. To no longer care, no longer feel. To become someone you never wanted to be. You've got to tell him why, Mark. You've got to tell him why.

(Lights fade to black.)

End of Act One

ACT II

Scene One

(TIME: The next day. Early evening.)

(The room is empty. The room phone begins ringing. The front door opens and **MARK** *enters, hears the phone and picks it up.)*

MARK. Hello. Oh, hi Wendy.

(Takes out his cell phone)

Oh, I guess I forgot to turn it on. They asked us to turn it off at the hospital. What's up, anything wrong? Good. Yes, yes, I'm fine and things down here are actually going very well. It started out a little rough but it seems to have calmed down. I wish you could have come down here. You wouldn't recognize your mother. The bloating is almost entirely gone from her face… Well, I thought you'd be interested.

Danny? He's fine. Listen, did you know he was having sex? What do you mean, so what? His girlfriend has missed her period. What do you mean, so what? Damn it, having sex comes with a lot of responsibilities. It's not just a fun thing. No, I haven't become a Republican, I'm trying to be a concerned parent. Think about it. He's only sixteen. Wendy, if you say "so what" one more time I'm hanging up.

What? Yes, actually we're getting along great. We've had some very nice conversations. Oh, about this and that. I'm sure if you ask him, he'll fill you in on everything. My memory's not that sharp anymore and frankly I'm not ready to re-live many of those moments again. I'll have him call you. He went to pick up some sandwiches for us. How's Brian and his family? Good.

MARK. *(cont.)* Listen, here's something I've been thinking about. When your mother comes home, what do you think of a little welcome home party for her? I know she'd love that. What do you mean you're busy? I didn't even set a date. Listen, you and your brother have got to let things go… Well, like the past. Why don't we look at this as a fresh new beginning? What do you mean you don't want to? You've got to stop being so damn negative. This is a very positive situation and good things are going to come from it. Okay, okay. I'm not going to get into that now. But, look, I've learned a lot here and when I get back I want to have a family meeting about how we all need to deal with her when she comes home. What do you mean you're too busy? Damn it Wendy, I'm looking for a little support here.

Okay, Okay. I'll talk to you when you have more time. Yeah, yeah, I told you, I'm fine. At least I was until I got this call. Look, when I get back we'll have dinner and we'll continue this discussion… Okay, then we'll just have dinner. Yeah. Thanks for calling. I love you too. Bye.

(Hangs up)

Jesus.

*(**DANNY** enters carrying a restaurant take out bag. He is wearing a Wonder Woman t-shirt.)*

DANNY. Here we are. Two cheeseburgers…

(Takes two cheeseburgers out of the bag)

…and for a very special occasion, presto! Two cold Buds.

(He produces two cans of beer.)

MARK. How did you get those?

DANNY. It's the old story. Money talks. The liquor store was right next to Wong's so I got one of the guys there to buy them for me.

MARK. And what's this special occasion?

DANNY. Jenny got her P-E-R-I-O-D.

MARK. Thank G-O-D. I hope you learned something from this experience.

DANNY. Like what?

MARK. Next time you want to have sex think about the possible results.

DANNY. That's the trouble. I do think about the results. The results are great. That's what makes me want to keep having sex.

MARK. Sometimes when I talk to you I feel like I should have legal counsel.

(They begin eating.)

DANNY. I was starving. Just what the hell was it they served at the hospital this afternoon?

MARK. I think it was some sort of turkey loaf.

DANNY. Really? I wonder how they got it to turn blue.

MARK. Your sister just called.

DANNY. Oh nice, how is she?

MARK. Totally disinterested.

DANNY. Well, she's obviously interested in you or else she wouldn't have called.

MARK. I guess so.

(Positive)

Well, what do you think?

DANNY. About what?

MARK. About today. How do you think it went?

DANNY. I guess okay.

MARK. Do you see a difference?

DANNY. In what?

MARK. In her?

DANNY. Do you?

MARK. Of course. Don't you?

DANNY. Yeah, I guess.

MARK. She's much calmer.

DANNY. Do you think so?

MARK. Yes, don't you?

DANNY. Yeah, I guess.

MARK. Your enthusiasm is overwhelming.

DANNY. Doing the best I can.

MARK. I was hoping I wouldn't ask you this because it's none of my business and if you don't want to tell me you don't have to. The fifteen minutes they gave you to be alone with her, how did it go?

DANNY. Fine.

MARK. What did you talk about?

DANNY. Nothing.

MARK. You must have said something?

DANNY. I did. When I saw her I said, "Hi mom."

MARK. And what did she say?

DANNY. Nothing. I guess she was still pissed off about yesterday.

MARK. Did you at least kiss her?

DANNY. No. I never kiss her. Not in the last five or six years.

MARK. I didn't know that. Did she try to kiss you?

DANNY. No. She never kisses me. We just don't kiss. We have a non-kissing relationship.

MARK. So what did you do for those fifteen minutes with her?

DANNY. I told you. Nothing. We just sat there.

MARK. You just sat?

DANNY. Yes.

MARK. You didn't talk?

DANNY. No.

MARK. Wasn't that uncomfortable?

DANNY. Not really.

MARK. Jesus. Did she say anything about your t-shirt?

DANNY. No. Why should she?

MARK. Well, as a young girl she loved Wonder Woman. She told me that once so that's why I bought the Wonder Woman t-shirts. I thought seeing it might give her a lift.

DANNY. She didn't say anything.

MARK. Nothing?

DANNY. Nope.

MARK. For fifteen minutes you two just sat there and said nothing.

DANNY. Yeah. Until it was time to go.

MARK. What happened then?

DANNY. I just got up and said nice talking to you mom. Then she called me an asshole and then I left.

MARK. I'm sure she didn't mean it.

DANNY. I'm sure she did. To be honest Dad, she seemed in worse shape today than she was yesterday. I don't know what the hell you're seeing, but I'm still seeing one angry screwed up person.

MARK. Damn it. They must have told her.

DANNY. Told her what?

MARK. They want to keep her another three weeks.

DANNY. Great! And I mean that in a nice way.

MARK. No you don't.

DANNY. I do. I think it's a good thing. Not necessarily for the wine and drug industry, but for her it makes sense. The longer she's away from the booze and pills the longer she's away from the booze and pills. It's that simple.

MARK. I don't know. She had her heart set on coming home. I'm sure she's very disappointed.

DANNY. Even better. And I mean that in a nice way too. Maybe for once in her life she should know a little disappointment. It could be, excuse the expression, very sobering.

MARK. You're being a horse's ass again.

DANNY. Yeah, I'm pretty good at it, aren't I.

MARK. A bit too good. In any case, it's going to be a little difficult for her for a few days, so let's do our best not to aggravate the situation.

DANNY. Dad, I was waiting for a better time to tell you this, but I have a feeling there isn't going to be one. I've been doing a lot of thinking and I think it's best if I don't live at home anymore.

MARK. Are you serious?

DANNY. It's not healthy for her, it's not healthy for me.

MARK. No, I don't want to hear it. You can't. She'll be devastated.

DANNY. Come on, that's the last thing she'll be. She wasn't devastated when Brian left, she wasn't devastated when Wendy left. She was very happy to see them go.

MARK. Yeah, but you're the youngest. You're her favorite.

DANNY. I'm not her favorite. She has no favorites. She just hates me a little bit less.

MARK. No, it's not right. When Brian and Wendy left, they were old enough to go. You're not. Why are you hitting me with this now?

DANNY. I can't stay there anymore, Dad. I can't. Try to understand that.

MARK. I don't know what to say, how to handle this. Can't you at least wait until you finish high school?

DANNY. I'm sorry. I can't be around her anymore. If I do, you're going to have two basket cases on your hands.

MARK. Where will you stay?

DANNY. Wendy said I can stay with her.

MARK. She has a studio apartment.

DANNY. Maybe with your help we can get a bigger place. Otherwise I can stay with Jen's family.

MARK. They'd let you stay there?

DANNY. They're very progressive people. They're from New York.

MARK. I prefer you staying with Wendy.

DANNY. I thought you would.

MARK. When were you planning to go?

DANNY. Well, now that she's going to be here another three weeks there's no hurry, but I'd like to be gone before she gets home. I think it will make things a lot easier for everyone.

MARK. Please, Danny, things are going to change.

DANNY. Stop saying that. Will you please stop saying that. Things aren't going to change. She's not going to change and you're not going to change. You're both two very fucked up people and if I stay at home any longer I'll end up just as fucked up as the two of you. For Christ's sake Dad, when are you going to realize the woman is insane?

MARK. Yes, but that's the alcohol.

DANNY. No, no it's not. Maybe in the beginning it was, but now it's gone past that. She's insane because she is insane. Whether she sobers up or not, she's insane and she's going to stay that way. I saw it today. In her eyes, the anger, the meanness, it's all there. I don't care if she never has another drink, that craziness is never going to leave her and I don't want to be around it anymore.

MARK. Danny, I…

DANNY. Listen to me, Dad. Listen! Until I was twelve years old I hated you.

MARK. I didn't know that.

DANNY. Yes, I hated you because as far back as I could remember, she used to say things, about you, about the family. And I used to believe everything she told me. Everything.
She used to call Wendy trailer trash, a little whore, a tramp… Brian was a weakling, a daddy's boy who was never going to amount to anything.

MARK. He's a fine lawyer and she's very proud of him.

DANNY. She doesn't give a damn about him or Wendy or me or you either. She accused you of things, some things so sick it upsets me just thinking about it. She'd come into my room and tell me how you'd hit her and punch her, even though there was never a mark on her body. She told me how she had to stop you from beating us up all the time when we were small. Fucking sick, dad. And there were other things, a lot of other things.

MARK. It was the alcohol, Danny. It was the alcohol.

DANNY. It didn't matter what it was because I believed her. Then as I got older, I saw things for what they were. I began to argue with her. I started doubting her, calling her out on things. That's when she turned on me. Saying things to me that were so vicious, so fucking evil. One day during one of her drunken stupors, she said I wasn't your kid. I couldn't have been any more than eleven or twelve. How would you like living with that?

MARK. That's ridiculous. Of course you're mine. That much I know.

DANNY. Do you?

MARK. *(Firmly)* Yes! That much I know.

DANNY. Well, I don't. Till this day I'm not sure. Goddamn it Dad. She's a drunk and you're out of town a lot. All the times you'd call in the evening and she wasn't home, didn't that bother you?

MARK. She'd go to a movie or she'd be with some of her lady friends. She'd always tell me.

DANNY. She wasn't always at the movies and her friends weren't always ladies. You have no idea how often I wanted to tell you. But I knew how it would hurt you. And like you, I had hopes then too, that she would get better. That one day we would be the happy family you kept promising us we'd be. Well, now I don't believe anyone. Not her, not you, not this stupid program, not the stupid doctors, no one.

MARK. It's that goddamn job of mine. The long hours, the traveling, I should have left it long ago to be with her. She was lonely.

(He sinks to the bed.)

DANNY. Stop blaming yourself. It's her. It's strictly her.

(Looks at **MARK.** *From the look on his father's face he realizes something.)*

You knew, didn't you? You knew she was running around. You had to.

MARK. I knew. I didn't want to believe it. I didn't want to see it. That was my sickness.

DANNY. Didn't it bother you? Didn't it anger you?

MARK. More than you'll ever know.

DANNY. And you said nothing. You did nothing.

MARK. That's not true.

DANNY. *(Sarcastic)* Really? Just what the hell did you do?

MARK. I cried.

*(***DANNY*** looks at him with pity.)*

(Lights fade to black.)

Scene Two

(TIME: The middle of the night. The room is pitch black.)

*(Both **MARK** and **DANNY** are asleep. **MARK**'s cell phone begins ringing. **MARK** switches on the lamp and answers. **DANNY** lifts his head to hear the conversation.)*

MARK. Hello? Yes, this is he. What? Oh, my God.

DANNY. What happened?

MARK. *(To **DANNY**)* It's the hospital. Your mother's missing.

DANNY. *(Fed up)* Great!

MARK. *(On phone)* You checked everywhere? The grounds, the bathrooms? Did you call the police? How the hell does something like this happen?… What about her clothes? Her suitcase? Did she take any of that? What about the bus station? Is someone down there?

(Looks at watch)

Christ, it's three in the morning. You can't just let her roam around town. Well, goddamn it, keep looking. She's got to be somewhere around there.

(Hangs up)

Damn!

(Starts dressing)

DANNY. What are you going to do?

MARK. Get in my car and look for her. Who the hell knows where she is? All the bars are closed and there hasn't been a bus out of here since ten. She could be walking the streets.

DANNY. I'll go with you.

MARK. No. Stay by the phone. If anyone calls, get me on my cell.

DANNY. How the hell does anyone escape from that place? It's like a high security prison.

MARK. They don't know for sure. They think she could have been hiding in the cafeteria and when they were unloading a supply truck she slipped out. I'll call you as soon as I learn something. Jesus, did we need this?

DANNY. I didn't. But maybe you did.

MARK. And what is that supposed to mean?

DANNY. Once more it's about her. Twenty-four hours a day, the attention, the focus is all on her. And once again it's Dad to the rescue. I'm beginning to think you really enjoy that role. The shining knight to save the beautiful princess. But she's not the beautiful princess. Not anymore. She's the wicked queen and I don't know why you refuse to see that.

MARK. She's your mother goddamn it. She could be in danger. Show some concern. What do you expect me to do? There's a life at stake, Danny. Can't you get that through your head?

DANNY. All our lives have been at stake. Why can't you get that through your head?

Why can't you see we needed saving too? We're all covered with scars, Dad. Every one of us. Thanks to her, scars that will never, ever go away. Damn it, Dad! Don't you think I wanted to love her? Don't you think I needed to love her? Don't you think I wanted to have feelings for her the way every one I know has for their mother? My mother! My mother! My fucking ice cold hearted, hatred filled, selfish mother! But I don't and I can't. And that's the way it is and that's the way it'll always be because that's the way she made it, that's the way she wants it and why you can't see it is beyond me.

(**MARK** *looks at him, confused and not knowing what to think.*)

MARK. I need to go.

(**MARK**'s *cell phone rings. He answers.*)

Yes? Oh, God. Is she okay? She was? She was.

(Disappointed)

MARK. *(cont.)* Okay, okay. I'll get right down there. No, no. Please, let me pick her up. It'll be better. Yeah, yeah. Don't worry, I'll find it.

(Hangs up and sighs in relief)

She's at the Police Station. They found her passed out on a park bench. She'd been drinking.

DANNY. Where the hell did she get money for that? I thought the hospital confiscated everything when she checked in.

MARK. I gave her, her ATM card. She asked for it and I gave it to her. She said she'd just feel better if she had it in case of an emergency. There was no place in the hospital she could use it for anything bad and I didn't want to upset her by insinuating I didn't trust her, so I gave it to her. Shit! If there's a right way to go with her and a wrong way to go with her, I always manage to pick the wrong way. Again and again and again and again and once more I fucked up. Once more it's my own stupid, stupid, stupid, god damn fault.

DANNY. What are you talking about? What else is your fault?

(MARK sits on his bed, at this point too emotional to say anything. He shakes his head sadly.)

What else is your fault?

(There is still no answer. DANNY rises and puts his hand on his father's shoulder.)

Don't worry. I'll go with you Dad.

(He sits down next to his father and puts his arm around him.)

(Lights fade to black.)

Scene Three

(TIME: That morning, about 7AM.)

*(**OLDER GWEN** is in **MARK**'s bed, covered up and asleep. **MARK** sits by her side and strokes her head. **DANNY**'s duffel bag is packed and on his bed. His guitar case is near the door. **DANNY** enters.)*

DANNY. There's a bus leaving in a half an hour. If I leave now I can make it.

MARK. Sure.

DANNY. How is she?

MARK. I think she'll be okay.

DANNY. Yeah. Well, for your sake, I hope so. I really think you need to send her back. It really is her only chance and yours too.

MARK. I know.

DANNY. But you won't.

MARK. I don't know.

DANNY. No, you won't.

MARK. Will you be home when I get there?

DANNY. No. I'll be at Wendy's. I think it will work out fine. It's only ten minutes further away from school.

MARK. Are you sure it's the right thing?

DANNY. At this point it's the only thing.

MARK. I'm sorry I got you into all this. God, I have screwed everything up. I shouldn't have made you come down here.

DANNY. I love you Dad, but there's more to the story, isn't there? There's something you don't want to talk about.

MARK. You won't understand.

DANNY. Then damn it, make me understand. I need to know.

MARK. Yes. Yes you do. Look at her. We are looking at two different people. I don't see what you see. You don't see what I see.

DANNY. I see a selfish, deteriorated drunk who never gave a damn about anyone and will probably die a hopeless alcoholic.

MARK. And I see the beautiful young woman who I fell madly in love with. The other night when I said everyone has one great love in their life, yes, she was mine. But you were right. I wasn't hers. Hers was a guy named Steve.

DANNY. I'm sorry. I didn't know that.

MARK. Why would you? She was twenty, he was twenty one. She was desperately in love. They lived together for a couple of years. She wanted marriage and a family, but like lots of guys his age, he wasn't settled with a job, a direction and for whatever reason it all fell apart.

Not long after that, we met at a party. I fell in love with her the minute I saw her. Don't ask me why. I just did. She had the saddest eyes. I was eight years older than she was and had everything Steve didn't have. A career, self confidence, money. She told me everything and even though it was obvious then she was still in love with this Steve I was determined to make all the sadness she had go away. I was determined to make her forget him.

We had such fun together. Restaurants, night clubs, rock concerts, trips to Hawaii, the Caribbean, and wine and champagne cocktails and rum coolers… It was the most wonderful time for me and I honestly believed for her too. Slowly the sadness seemed to leave her.

We were married six months after we met. Just a simple little ceremony with a few friends. We didn't even have family there. And she cried. She cried through the whole damn thing. Everyone, including me, thought it was because she was happy. Years later, looking back, I realized the truth. She was crying for him.

For the next few years there was no happier man on Earth than me. I had married the woman I loved and knew I would love forever. We had Brian and then

Wendy. She was everything I wanted her to be, a loving wife, a good mother and beautiful, so beautiful.

But then slowly that sadness that she once had began to creep back. Conversation with her became difficult. She didn't seem interested in me, the kids, nothing.

And then I realized that if she had a glass or two of wine with dinner it seemed to make the evening better, get her smiling again. Once more I thought everything was going to be wonderful.

Unfortunately, a glass or two soon became three or four. And it began to escalate. A cocktail before dinner. Then one after dinner. Her personality began to change. She became angry, irritable, sometimes mean. I wasn't stupid. I knew what was happening. It was the damn booze. And I knew I had to stop things and so help me, Danny, I had every intention of doing so.

But then one day, looking over a phone bill, I discovered there were several calls made to some town up in Oregon. It was Steve. She tracked him down. When I confronted her she told me everything. She still loved him and he said he still loved her.

She had no plans to leave me but there was little doubt in my mind that one day she would. So I made a decision. I would rather have her drunk than not at all. I hired someone to come in and help with the house and you kids. I made it even easier for her to keep drinking and drinking and drinking.

The phone calls between her and Steve continued and eventually they arranged to see each other. They had dinner, and of course drinks, and it went exactly the way I thought it would. She saw the man she loved with all her heart, but he saw someone he didn't know anymore, someone he could never love again.

For several months afterwards she tried calling him but he wouldn't take her calls. It was over. She was now mine for good. I had won. But I never saw her happy again.

MARK. *(cont.)* I thought when you came along it would make a difference. It didn't.

I once read a book that asked the question, is it better *to* love or *to be* loved. For both of us the answer was always *to* love. I loved her, she loved him and for the two of us, that's the way it was always going to be.

DANNY. Jesus. I knew you two had some kind of story. I didn't expect this.

MARK. I know. I didn't either. What you see lying in that bed, I caused. I did this to her. I turned her into what she is and I've got to fix her. I've got to get her back to who she was. I owe her that much. I've got to fix what I broke. I can't let it end this way. I can't.

*(***OLDER GWEN*** starts to stir.)*

OLDER GWEN. Mark!

MARK. Yes, I'm here.

OLDER GWEN. I'm sorry. They wanted to keep me longer.

MARK. I know.

OLDER GWEN. I couldn't do it. It hurt too much. It just hurt too much.

MARK. I know.

OLDER GWEN. Please don't make me go back. I'll quit on my own. I promise. Don't make me go back.

MARK. I won't. I promise I won't.

OLDER GWEN. I'll quit, Mark. I'll change. I know I will this time. Don't make me go back.

MARK. No. No I won't. Danny 's here. Do you want to say hello?

(She's back asleep.)

Gwen! Gwen!

*(To **DANNY**)*

She's asleep.

DANNY. Yeah. I think passed out is a little more accurate. Well, I better go.

MARK. Wait.

(Takes out some money and hands it to him)

Take this. We'll work out some financial arrangement when I get back.

DANNY. *(Puts the money in his pocket)* Thanks Dad. Good luck.

MARK. Good luck to you son.

*(**MARK** hugs **DANNY** then returns to his wife's bedside. **DANNY** picks up his bag and guitar. He looks at his father and then takes a deep breath.)*

DANNY. I... I didn't really know what I wanted from this week with you. It had to be more than driving your car down here. I understand what it was now. I always wondered when you gave us up for her, if you were really aware of what you were doing. If you really knew what living with her was doing to us, to me, to Wendy, to Brian. I needed to know that. I see now, whether you did or you didn't, didn't really matter. It was only her you were concerned about. All the time, it was only her.

MARK. I swear Danny, I didn't mean for it to be that way.

DANNY. Do you know what really sucks about our lives? It seems we were always trying to protect you, but you didn't really give a rat's ass about us. You chose to spend your life trying to save a goddamn mean, selfish, miserable drunk over three helpless kids. You let every day of our lives with that woman be just as rotten as yours. How sad is that and what a waste. That woman robbed us of our childhood, Dad. All three of us. And you just stood by and let it happen.

*(**DANNY** goes to the door and opens it.)*

MARK. Danny!

*(**DANNY** turns to his father.)*

You need to truly love someone, to really understand.

DANNY. Yes, but that doesn't make it right. It doesn't make it right! You should have loved *us* more.

(**DANNY** *exits, closing the door behind him.* **MARK** *is stunned for a moment. He rises and calls after* **DANNY**.)

MARK. But I did love you! I swear I did love you! All three of you!

(*Starts for the door*)

Danny, wait!

(**OLDER GWEN** *calls weakly from the bed.*)

OLDER GWEN. Mark! Mark!

(**MARK** *turns to her.*)

MARK. I'm here.

OLDER GWEN. Please, don't make me go back. Please.

MARK. No. No, I promise, I won't.

(*She raises her hand to him to hold. He looks at the door then back at* **GWEN**. *Once again he knows he's faced with a decision. He lowers his head and then sits at* **OLDER GWEN***'s side, takes her hand and holds it. She is fast asleep again. The room darkens.* **YOUNG GWEN** *appears behind him.*)

YOUNG GWEN. One day I'll quit, Mark. I'll be that same person you fell in love with. You know that. One day I will.

MARK. Yes, I know.

YOUNG GWEN. One day it will all be fine again.

MARK. Yes, yes it will.

YOUNG GWEN. You still love me, don't you Mark?

MARK. Yes. I still love you.

YOUNG GWEN. One day I'll quit, Mark. I will. You believe that, don't you?

MARK. Yes, I believe that. We both need to believe that. It's all we have left.

(**MARK** *kisses* **OLDER GWEN**'s *hand and then rests his head on it.*)

(*The lights fade to black.*)

The End

PROPS

ACT I

Scene 1
Medium sized structured suitcase with MARK's clothes
Nylon duffel bag with DANNY's clothes
Guitar in a guitar case
Small hotel hand towel
DANNY's cell phone

Scene 2
None

Scene 3
Six Superhero t-shirts for **DANNY**
    2 Batman, 2 Superman, 2 Wonder Woman
Bag for t-shirts
Take out menu
MARK's cell phone

Scene 4
Bottle of wine
Wine glass

Scene 5
None

Scene 6
None

ACT II

Scene 1
Restaurant bag containing 2 cheeseburgers, 2 Cans of
    Budweiser beer

Scene 2
MARK's cell phone

Scene 3
None

COSTUMES

ACT I

Scene 1
DANNY – Jeans, sneakers, rock band t-shirt
MARK – Slacks, sweater, loafers

Scene 2
MARK – Pajama bottoms, white undershirt
YOUNG GWEN – White night gown.

Scene 3
DANNY – Jeans, Budweiser t-shirt, sneakers
MARK – Slacks, shirt, light jacket

Scene 4
DANNY – Boxer shorts
OLDER GWEN – White nightgown
MARK – Pajama bottoms, white undershirt
YOUNG GWEN – White nightgown

Scene 5
MARK – Slacks, shirt, light jacket
DANNY – Jeans, Miller beer t-shirt, sneakers

Scene 6
MARK – Pajama bottoms, white undershirt
OLDER GWEN – White nightgown

ACT II

Scene 1
MARK – Slacks, shirt
DANNY – Jeans, Wonder Woman t-shirt, sneaker

Scene 2
MARK – Pajama bottoms, white undershirt
DANNY – Boxer shorts
MARK – Slacks, shirt, light jacket

Scene 3
MARK – Slacks, shirt from previous scene
OLDER GWEN – One of **MARK**'s white t-shirts
DANNY – Jeans, t-shirt, jacket
YOUNG GWEN – White nightgown

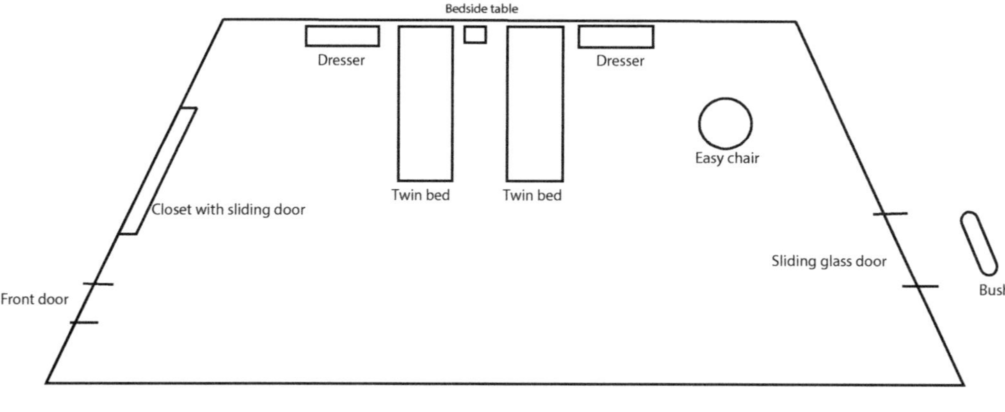

Fixing Gwen Set Design